SPACE PATROL DELTA

Dalmatian Press, LLC, 2006. All Rights Reserved. Printed in the U.S.A.
The DALMATIAN PRESS name and logo are trademarks of Dalmatian Press, LLC, Franklin, Tennessee 37067.
No part of this book may be reproduced or copied in any form without written permission of Dalmatian Press,
BVS Entertainment, Inc., and BVS International N.V.

15570 Power Rangers SPD: Space Patrol Delta

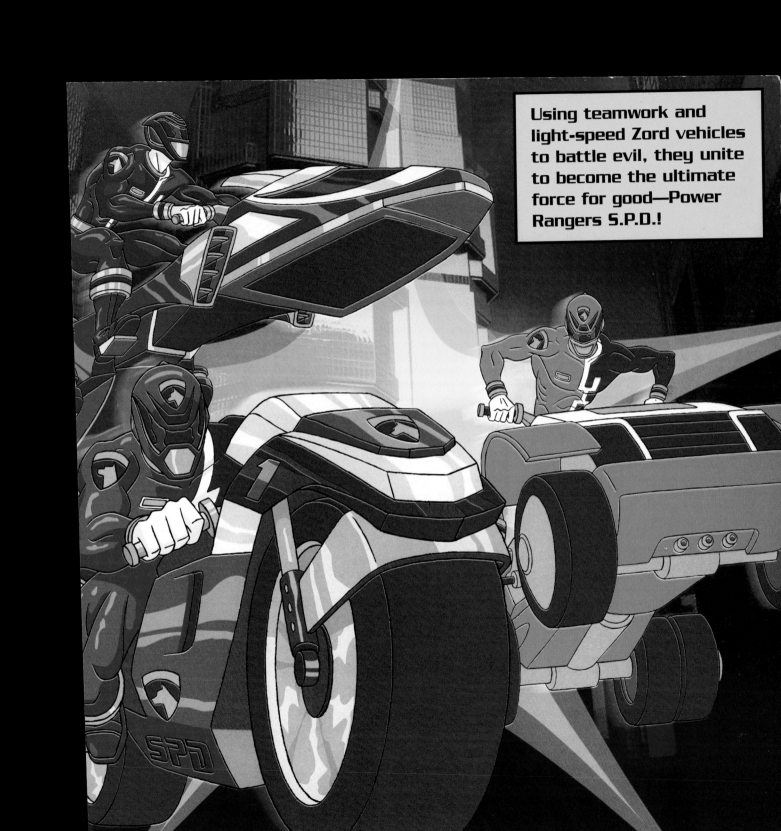

Using teamwork and light-speed Zord vehicles to battle evil, they unite to become the ultimate force for good—Power Rangers S.P.D.!

Jack Landers is the Red S.P.D. Ranger, the squad leader. He is able to molecularize himself and pass through solid objects.

"Sky" Tate is the Blue S.P.D. Ranger, the son of a former Red Ranger. He is able to create force fields.

Bridge Carson, a master mechanic with psychic powers, is the Green S.P.D. Ranger.

The Pink S.P.D. Ranger is Sydney Drew—the baton wielding beauty!

The Yellow S.P.D. Ranger is "Z" Delgado, who can clone herself.

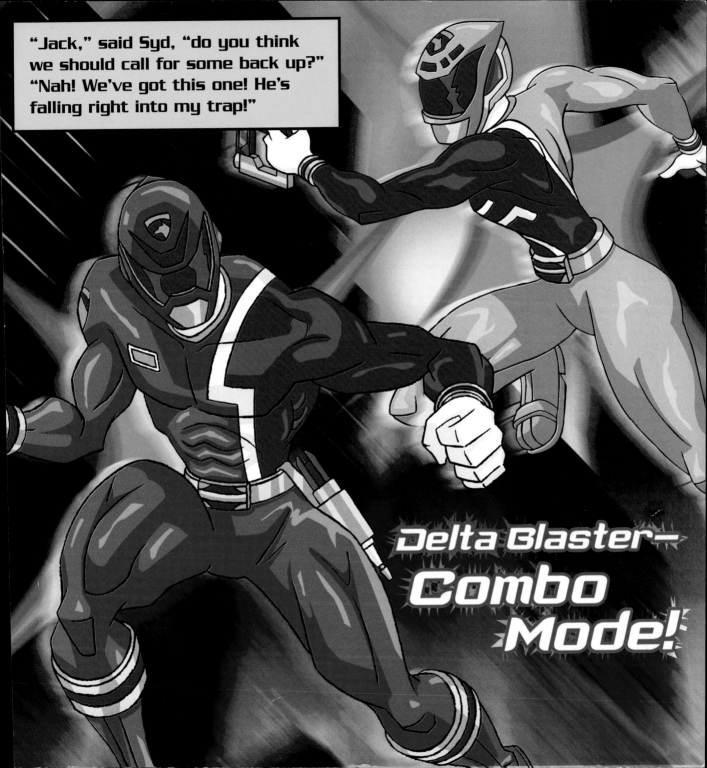

With the defeat of the Krybot, yet another call was sent for the S.P.D. Rangers.

S.P.D. Emergency
Morphers in Ignition Mode!

The Rangers were dispatched from Delta Base in their Squad Runners—elite emergency vehicles.

Piloted by the Rangers, the Delta Squad Runners are equipped with state-of-the-art lasers, lasso-throwing capabilities, and blasters.

Power Rangers— to the rescue!

Back in the city, a huge robot was drilling proton spikes into the ground. The next spike—a mega neutron spike—would cause an earthquake on a Quasar 3 level!

Delta Squad Megazord!

The Rangers were called to Sector 4, Area 6, where they saw the Shadow Ranger standing over the defeated Benaag.

"Who is that Ranger?" asked Jack. "It's—it's Commander Cruger!" they all called out in amazement.

Containment Mode!

Benaag was reduced to a mere squirming image on a Containment Card—and taken back to Command Base.

Watching the scene from his lair, Gruumm grumbled, "Yes, I have failed this time, for I have underestimated the Power Rangers."

Once again, through Discipline, Control, and Teamwork...
Justice prevails!